Enoch Conklin

**An Interesting History of Florida and the Famous Tarpon**

**Springs**

the new health resort of Florida

Enoch Conklin

**An Interesting History of Florida and the Famous Tarpon Springs**
*the new health resort of Florida*

ISBN/EAN: 9783337369514

Printed in Europe, USA, Canada, Australia, Japan

Cover: Foto ©Andreas Hilbeck / pixelio.de

More available books at **www.hansebooks.com**

AN

# INTERESTING HISTORY

OF

# FLORIDA

AND THE FAMOUS

# TARPON SPRINGS.

## THE NEW HEALTH RESORT

OF

# FLORIDA.

# FLORIDA.

UST before the Spaniards under Cortez began their great conquest of Mexico in 1520, the French sent out an expedition for the purpose of appropriating some of the newly discovered land of America to itself. Ponce de Leon with his expedition, discovered the land of the Floridas in 1512. He landed on the east coast near the St. Johns river where St. Augustine now stands, and named the country *Florida*, on account of the rich and fertile growths, which everywhere met his gaze. It was at this place where he afterwards founded the Huguenot colony, which spread and flourished in these parts for upwards of 40 years; and of whose persecution afterwards by the Spaniards, history furnishes another thrilling account of the religious terrors of the 16th century.

In 1520, when Cortez opened the conquest of Mexico, Luke Vasques de Ayllon in the same year, equipped two ships and sailed from Hispaniola for the contemptuous and short-sighted purpose of capturing and placing the innocent natives into bondage. Arriving on the east coast, he invited the Indians on board, and when secured, he set sail for St. Domingo and sold them into slavery.

In 1527, Charles V., of Spain, commissioned Pamphilo de Narvaez to conquer Florida. Arriving at Tampa Bay on the west coast, about 30 miles below where Tarpon Springs now stands, he issued a proclamation that he would destroy all the Indians if they did not acknowledge the

# THE "TARPON"

IS THE NAME OF THE LARGE

# NEW WINTER RESORT HOTEL,

## OF FLORIDA.

Lately Built on the Lake Butler Villa Company's Grounds at

# TARPON SPRINGS,

## ON THE WEST COAST OF FLORIDA. •

# IT IS ONE OF THE FINEST ON THE COAST

From Tallahassee to the Southern extremity of Florida.

It was named after the game fish of that name which abound on the Gulf near its very doors, in the Streams and Bayous at the Springs.

## It Contains 50 Rooms!

### ITS TABLE IS FURNISHED WITH

# All the Delicacies the Season & Market Affords

## HUNTING, FISHING,

Yachting, Bathing, and all the Sports the Seekers after Pleasure ask for, are found at its very doors. As for climate, it is well known that the temperature is beginning to attract the attention of persons of the East or Atlantic Coast.

sovereignty of the Pope and the King. He then marched north through Hillsborough and Hernando counties, on to Pensacola in search of the Mississippi River, where he lost his life and those of all his men in trying to cross it in a storm.

In 1538, another commission of the same nature was given to Hernando De Soto to "conquer all Florida," with a promise that he should receive the title of Marquis of all the lands he so conquered. In 1539, De Soto landed at the Bay of Tampo—about the same spot where the Narvaez entered. This Bay was then called under the Spanish title, Espiritu Santo. De Soto had with him on this occasion about 600 of his best soldiers. On his arrival he proclaimed to the natives that his expedition was for "God alone." It seems that from this date the great intrigues for religious persecutions began. Landing for the purpose of conquest and gain he claimed his object was for their souls' welfare. At this time, Santander, in a letter to the Emperor, came greatly to De Soto's aid. This letter kindled a religious fire and fervor, which increased until the Priests in Cortez's army destroyed, in their great historic fire, the last remaining archives of the Aztec Empire in Mexico. We give Santander's letter below:

"It is lawful that your majesty, like a good Shepherd, appointed by the hand of the eternal Father, should tend and lead out your sheep, since the Holy Spirit has shown spreading pastures whereon are feeding lost sheep which have been snatched away by the dragon, the demon. These pastures are the new world wherein is comprised Florida, now in possession of the demon, and here he makes himself adored and revered. This is the land of promise possessed by idolators; this is the land promised by the eternal Father to the faithful, since we are commanded by God in the Holy Scriptures to take it from them, being idolators;

and by reason of their idolatry and sin, to put them all to the knife, leaving no living thing, save maidens and children; their cities robbed and sacked, their walls and houses leveled to the earth."

On the strength of their letter, De Soto was permitted to enslave the inhabitants for his own use and service. Santander further, selected four places in Florida, which, from the fertility of the soil and other favorable conditions, he recommended to the King to at once lay hold upon. The country for miles round about Tampa Bay, and where De Soto was at that time, was one of the four locations. The others were, Pensacola, Tallahassee, and the country about the mouth of the St. John's River. De Soto favored the west coast.

In 1565, Melendez in his commission from King of Spain, to Christianize the natives of Florida, usurped his right and attacked also the French Huguenot colony. The religious fire and fervor created by Santander's letter seems not to have stopped with the native Indians; for Melendez proclaimed to the French Huguenots that if they too did not surrender to the church and to Spain, he would kill every one of them. Refusing, they were, true to the temerity of the Spaniards, completely extirpated. The Spaniards attacked a fleet of Huguenots off their settlement at sea. The Huguenots were beaten under Ribault, who was driven down the coast and lost. Melendez then attacked the land forces at Fort Carolina on the St. John's River, captured the fort, and hung all the French who manned it. He then went in search of those who escaped down the coast; and, having overtook them at Matanzas inlet, he assured them that if they would surrender they would be pardoned. No sooner had they surrendered, however, than they were taken behind the sand hills of the coast and massacred. France and England were indignant, but nothing was done until

A War Dance of the Ancient Florida Indians

the great French chevalier, Dominique de Gourgues, who had served against the Spaniards in Italy, fitted out two ships, attacked and took the French forts with the Spaniards in them, and hung all the soldiery—not as Spaniards, but as traitors, murderers and robbers. He afterwards demolished the forts and returned to France.

Until the purchase of Florida by the United States in 1821, the Spaniards continued to hold the country for a period of about 250 years, except for a term of 20 years, in which it was ceded to England—from 1763 to 1783.

# FLORIDA.

—o—

# THE WEST COAST

### AND

## What it is! Where it is!

## How to Get There!

#### And all about the rich country's new

## PLEASURE RESORTS,

#### BETWEEN

## DISSTON AND CEDAR KEYS,

### ON THE GULF OF MEXICO.

The Steamer Gov. Safford Leaving the Wharf at Tarpon Springs.

# TARPON SPRINGS.

Tarpon Springs is situated upon a system of indentures of the Gulf of Mexico, near the mouth of the Anclote River, about 30 miles north of the bay of Tampa, and 60 miles south of Cedar Keys. The system of small bays, rivulets, lakes, etc., which are so beautifully characteristic of Florida, is complete here.

One most admirable and salient feature of this section of the west coast, is that for several miles north and south of Tarpon Springs, the country has a general elevation as you proceed inland. Reaching some of the higher elevations you find imbedded in some beautifully foliaged plateau, the system of lakes which are destined to convert this region into villa plots and residences which will surpass any thing yet seen in the State. Landing on the wharf just below one of the natural springs in which this particular location abounds, you find that Tarpon avenue has descended a gentle grade to your very feet, giving you a most pleasant reception.

Looking up through the rich foliage, with the stately forest growths on either side, you catch just a glimpse of the sentiments afterwards enjoyed in your rides to the lakes, to which this avenue leads. It is not all sentiment either. The element of air invigorates the body as the pleasures of sight does the mind, and your senses at once account to nature for her sweet influences.

In driving up this avenue you see, at short intervals, beautiful crystal lakes winking and blinking at you through the trees in the bright scintillating sun light, until you reach

## LAKE BUTLER,

one of the beauty spots of creation. This is an introduction to the wonderful water system of this section of country, which is a great boon to it. It is owing to this great water supply that one is compelled, however warm the days, to sleep under a blanket at night.

The gentle elevation of the land as you recede from the coast waters, secures this place as a natural Sanitarium. In point of its drainage it is perfect. Its air, and the aroma from its resinous Pines, and other smaller growths, give vigor and an embracing life to the physical man, while the medical qualities of its Springs as a remedial agency, are unsurpassed.

It is well known that the belief was entertained among the Spaniards that a spring could be found, the waters of which would restore the vigor of youth to age, and perpetuate life eternally, and much of their explorations were devoted in efforts to make this discovery.

Whether the Congress Springs are these Springs, we do not presume to say. We leave that for each one to determine by his own experiments. The investigation of them will be pleasant pastimes while there.

The rapid growth of the town springing so spasmodically into existence shows the merit of its selection. The location was chosen not until those who located it had traversed the whole State. It was located about January 1st, 1883. In 1884, the requirements of the town induced a steamboat company to form, and the splendid excursion steamer, "Gov. Safford," was put on in November to ply between Disstou and Cedar Keys. From Cedar Keys, one has

THE TARPON SPRINGS HOTEL.

the Palace Car to New York direct, and to all parts of the country.

A school house had been erected.

A Hack line had been established to run south to Tampa, giving tourists a romantic ride through the forests, and along side the crystal lakes of Florida.

Two Hotels had been built, giving fare equal to New York or San Francisco, at rates lower than at the former place.

Telegraphic facilities had been established. Stores had been built, and saw mills started.

# TARPON SPRINGS.

The place is admirably located for excursion trips in any direction, If the tourist comes from Cedar Keys north, he can then go to Tampa south, by one of the pleasantest

## COACH RIDES THROUGH THE WOODS

### TO BE FOUND ANYWHERE.

If he comes by way of the south, and has seen Tampa, he can take the steamer,

### "GOVERNOR SAFFORD,"

#### AND ENJOY A

## SIX HOURS' SAIL ON THE GULF TO CEDAR KEYS.

East and West give equally pleasant results, and of a varied nature. To the east a romantic park-like ride brings you

## TO LAKE BUTLER,

A scene to be remembered all your life.

To the West takes you among innumerable

## ISLANDS AND BAYS

out to the full fledged Gulf, harboring as it does at certain seasons, the great sponge fleets of the South seas. It is estimated that one hundred thousand dollars worth of sponges are annually taken by this fleet.

# TO THE ANGLER.

Nature seems to have made this spot with the tacit understanding with all human kind, that he who was born with a spirit of the angler in him, should certainly visit it. Fishing in these waters is something like crabbing on the Harlem Flats at New York in the height of the season. The only difference is that the crabs there have their season; while to the fishing here, with the exception of some few species perhaps, there is no season. From January to December you may throw the line. Let the green turtle epicures come down here, and we'll give them a "deal." The hotels at Tampa set oysters on the tables continually as a relish, just as the hotels north furnish chow-chow or pickles.

The English Capt. Bernard Romans in his " Concise Natural History of Florida," says:

" The whole of the west coast of East Florida is covered with fishermen's huts and flakes; these are built by the Spanish fishermen from Havana, who come annually to this coast to the number of thirty sail, and one or two visit Rio d'Ais, or Indian River, and other places on the east coast. The principal fish here, of which the Spaniards make up their cargoes, is the red drum, called in East Florida a bass. They also salt a quantity of fish which they call pompanos, for which they get a price three times as high as for other fish. A few soles, sea trout, and the roe of mullet and black drum make up the remainder of their cargoes. These roes are dried and smoked, and used instead of caviare by the Spaniards, who are very fond of them."

Yachting and Fishing Grounds at Tarpon Springs

Again he says:—

"It abounds so much in fish, that a person may sit on the bank and stick them with a knife or sharp stick, as they swim by. I have frequently shot from four to twelve mullets at one shot; nay, our boys used to go alongside the vessel in the boat and kill the catfish with a hatchet. In St. Augustine, the fishermen used to allow people who brought a real (12½ cents) to take as many fish as they pleased out of the boats."

Dr. C. J. Kenworthy, author of "Fishing with the Fly," says:

"Lake Butler, a short distance from the hotel, affords good fishing for Black Bass."

[The hotel above alluded to is the Tarpon Springs Hotel ]

THE TARPON SPRINGS HOTEL, is the headquarters for these Great Fishing and Hunting Grounds, being within the company's domains.

Speaking of many other conditions of this location, the Doctor further says: * * * * "and last though not least, a greater variety of fish that will take the fly, than in any other section of the Union."

Fishes of the Gulf Coast of Florida caught at Tarpon Springs.

# DESCRIPTION OF THE FAMOUS FISH OF FLORIDA.

THE RED SNAPPER:—Truly a sportsman's fish, abounds along the west coast. Size at and about Tarpon, averaging from 3 lbs. to 8 lbs. They are a shy fish, but will snap savagely at your bait, and will give you a lively and interesting chase if you have a good line, and plenty of it; and after you return home will heighten the satisfaction you had in taking him by giving you a savory relish. This fish is good moonlight sport, as it feeds well at night.

THE SALT WATER CAT-FISH:—Here we have a fish, which, though not largely eaten by the people of Florida, has a firm and well flavored flesh, and furnishes good sport for the inexperienced angler. It "takes every thing within its reach" liberally; and in some cases are so plenty in places, that you may drop your hook among them, without bait, and hook them in the side, breast, and all parts of the body.

THE MULLET:—This, although not a game fish, is of a more essential interest to mankind, as it is a food fish and is also the principal bait for all the angling fish of Florida. This species is so prolific, it seems the more you kill the more there is remains—like the emphatic mosquito. The lakes, rivers and bays swarm with them; often it would seem that your boat would be obstructed by a shoal of them ahead of you in the river. They never take the bait and have to be netted. They furnish food for all the greater variety of all the other fish; afford much amusement in leaping into the air, and performing their antics; they were the favorite dish of the ancient Romans.

THE SHEEPSHEAD:—Can be taken in droves and with ready bait.

THE TARPON:—This is decidedly a game fish. With scales as big and as bright as a silver dollar, leaping and making chaos and commotion on the surface of a summer bay or Bayou. Well, suffice to say, that when you succeed in "bringing in" one of these, weighing any thing over 20 lbs. the Tarpon Springs Hotel will illuminate in your honor—always.

The scales of this fish are used for Florida jewelry.

THE POMPANO:—The sweetest food fishes of the west coast. To enjoy a sweetest morsel of the finny tribe, however, one must catch, cook and eat one of these fish at their native home.

THE SALT WATER TROUT:—This fish affords good sport on the hook, and gives corresponding satisfaction in its delicious flavor. It will not keep; but cooked and eaten at once is one of the greatest of delicacies. You must go to Florida to enjoy him.

It is known that all fish caught on the Florida coast, may be eaten, except perhaps the Hog-fish, and of this even many claim it, a safe and savory edible.

The following fish are plentiful throughout the coast.

| | |
|---|---|
| Kingfish, | Angle fish, |
| Mullet, | Red Drum, |
| Grouper, | Black Drum, |
| Red Snapper, | Parrotfish. |
| Pompanos, | Hogfish. |
| Jewfish, | Catfish. |
| Bluefish, | Black Bass, |
| Blackfish, | Channel Bass, |
| Sheepshead, | Ladyfish, |
| Tarpon, | Bream, |
| Silverfish, | Sea Trout. |
| Rockfish, | Cavalli, |
| Salt Water Trout | |

And many other smaller and delicious varieties.

# WITH THE SALE OF

# Four Millions of Acres

## OF

# CHOICE FLORIDA LANDS,

### TO WHAT IS KNOWN AS

# THE DISSTON COMPANY,

HAMILTON DISSTON, Esq.;       Ex. Gov. A. P. K. SAFFORD;
W. C. PARSONS, Esq.       and C. H. GROSS, Esq.

# HAVE OPENED TO THE WORLD

### THE NEW AND FAMED LANDS OF THE

# West Coast of Florida,

## BORDERING ON THE GULF OF MEXICO.

Headquarters of these new interests are at Tarpon Springs. Stop and glance at the Springs and see the lands of the

# Lake Butler Villa Company.

In speaking of this west Coast, Dr. J. C. Kenworthy, of Jacksonville, says: it is a " piscatorial incognito." And adds :

" The coast is shoal and can be navigated in a small boat.. The streams are numerous, and excellent camping-grounds' will be found on their banks. The shoal waters along the coast abound with ducks, the shores with beach birds, and the land with deer and turkeys. All the streams abound with black bass [southern trout], channel bass, cavalli, sheepshead, bream and sea trout. On these streams a fly rod would be found very useful."

# ORANGE CULTURE.

## ADAPTED TO THE WEST COAST.

The orange, as a product, has always stared the poor man in the face and out of countenance, from the fact that the tree took from 4 to 5 years to bear. He knew that there was a great market for vegetables which he might grow, and in which he might realize 30 per cent. from, on the capital he might lay out in an orange grove, while he was waiting for that grove to bear.

The great trouble was, until recently, he could not get his products to market. These facilities are now thoroughly given him by the great influx of railroads and steamboats, which are now going on. The great adaptability of the west coast bordering the Gulf of Mexico, for all citrus growths is now well established, and is being rapidly taken advantage of. Hillsborough and Hernando counties are especially noted. This whole section is being rapidly filled up. It is virgin soil; has just been put in the market, and the best orange and vegetable lands in the State can now be purchased here for the paltry sum of from $10 to $15 per acre.

As the mind requires something tangible, we give some figures below, which will aid one to more thoroughly calculate.

### COST OF A FIVE-ACRE ORANGE GROVE.

5 acres of best land $15 - - - - - - - - - $75.00
Breaking up and fencing $10 per acre - - - - - 50.00
300 trees and setting out—they should be seed-
    lings, 2 years old - - - - - - - - - - - 150.00
                                        $275.00

This is only an approximate. You can buy good orange land within five miles of shipping facilities for less—as low even as $10. Then again, you may have land which is less or more difficult to clear. But, to use round figures, $300 will show a five-acre Orange Grove nicely set out, and which, in three years, will give you a crop.

If you will set out your own trees, $50 may be taken off the above amount.

This having been accomplished, you proceed to put in your vegetables of which you realize, after 90 days from your investment, 40 per cent. profit, which continues until your oranges begin to come. The orange being a very hardy tree, and being set about 30 feet apart, leaves ample room for the whole area to be used for vegetables and under growths, until the orange get its growth; and, as every month in the year is used for planting some kind of vegetable, in Florida, the profit on an investment in an Orange Grove, may readily be seen dating from after the first 90 days, from the time of the purchase of the land.

Parties from the north are showing vigorous appreciation of these facts, and are forming companies for the purpose of raising vegetables to be shipped north in the winter. In the summer, vegetables of a semi-tropical nature will enable them to ship all the year round at fabulous prices. Bearing in mind that there is only one Florida; that the whole of the State is only 100 miles wide by 400 long; the value of these lands when all taken up can barely be computed. A thriving orange grove will net about $1,000 per acre annually.

We give, on pp. 28-29, a list of the vegetables which may be grown on the west coast, and the months they may be planted in.

# LEFT IN FLORIDA

## THIS YEAR THAN EVER BEFORE

### FOR THE PURCHASE OF THE

# Immense Orange Lands

## OF THE WEST COAST,

Which have been opened up for sale recently.

---

Read what a correspondent of the *New York Times* says, after a trip over this section last winter:

"The TIMES and I are still exploring strange countries, and when every New Yorker who can will be sailing boats and picking oranges in midwinter here on this Gulf coast of Florida, I shall take credit to myself for having been one of the first, at least, to bring this beautiful and quiet spot to the notice of the people. And I am glad to be able to write thus of it without feeling that I am making a tremendous puff for some wealthy corporation, for this west coast is virgin soil, owned principally by the State, and nobody is especially interested in bringing people to it."

# THE GREAT ORANGE QUESTION.

The question has been asked—"Won't orange raising be over done?" One might as well ask whether potatoes or corn will be over done. And more so, because there is an unlimited field for their growth. But not so with the orange. The Southern half of California and the peninsula of Florida is your limit. It has been estimated that if every inch of land in the whole United States, which would grow the orange, were planted with it, it would not necessitate a decline in prices. But there are two points to be considered:—

First: Regardless of price, people would use more of them because they would see more of them, and be brought in closer relation, upon the principle that merchandise will sell only in proportion as it is brought to the eyes and ears of the public. A man may have ever so good a thing, but if it was never brought to the notice of the public it would not sell.

A woman goes to market for the simple necessaries of life. She has no intention of buying any apples, grapes, oranges, or figs, but on walking through the market place, she espies some rosy cheeked apples. It occurs to her at once that "a few" of them would go nice in the evening or Sunday. Now she buys "a few" of them at least, regardless of price within reason. We venture to say that nine people out of ten thus bring home some little choice relish or morsel which was not on their list when they started out. And why? Simply, and for the one sole reason that *they saw it.*

This woman bought the apples because she *saw* them. She did not see any oranges. Now suppose that oranges were equally displayed with apples. How many, do you compute would be sold even if the prices were higher? The answer is, every orange that every inch of orange land in the United States could produce. But now comes in the sequel, and a pleasant one in the second point to be considered.

Secondly: It has been estimated that the orange crops could be made to stand a reduction of one-eighth their present cost, and still "pay." Oranges now bring, in Florida, two to three cents a piece at the groves. It has been shown they would pay at as low as one quarter of a cent each. The extreme high prices are, however, kept up by the orange grower, who, at these prices, reclines in all the luxuries of his grove, with more ease than grace, than that of your most opulent cotton grower further north.

But the reduction of the orange at a mere living profit it seems, will never be necessary, from the principle explained above. The demand increasing with their excessive exposure in the market, will more than balance any possible increase from the limited space of land we have to grow them in. No! It is a well proven problem that the orange grower will always live a comparative life of ease and luxury which ever way you compute.

# WHEN AND WHAT TO PLANT.

In *January*, plant Irish potatoes, peas, beets, turnips, cabbage, and all hardy or semi-hardy vegetables; make hot beds for pushing the more tender plants, such as melons, tomatoes, okra, egg-plants, etc.; set out fruit and other trees, and shrubbery.

*February*—Keep planting for a succession, same as in January; in addition, plant vines of all kinds, shrubbery, and fruit trees of all kinds, especially of the citrus family, snap beans, corn, bed sweet potatoes for draws and slips. Oats may also be still sown, as they are in previous months.

*March*—Corn, oats, and planting of February may be continued; transplant tomatoes, egg-plants, melons, beans, and vines of all kinds; mulberries, and blackberries are now ripening.

*April*—Plant as in March, except Irish potatoes, kohl rabi, turnips; continue to transplant tomatoes, okra, egg plants; sow millet, cow peas, for fodder; plant the butter bean, lady peas; dig Irish potatoes. Onions, beets, and usual early vegetables should be plenty for table.

*May*—Plant sweet potatoes for draws in beds; continue planting corn for table; snap beans, and cucumbers ought to be well forward for use; continue planting okra, egg plants, pepper, butter beans.

*June*—The heavy planting of sweet potatoes and cow peas is now in order; Irish potatoes, tomatoes, and a great variety of table vegetables are now ready, as also plums, early peaches, and grapes.

*July*—Sweet potatoes and cow peas are safe to plant, the rainy season being favorable; grapes, peaches and figs are in full season. Orange trees may be set out if the season is wet.

*August*—Finish up planting sweet potatoes and cow peas; sow cabbage, cauliflower, turnips for fall planting; plant kohl rabi and rutabagas; transplant orange trees and bud; last of month plant a few Irish potatoes and beans.

*September*—Now is the time to commence for the true winter garden—the garden which is commenced in the North in April and May. Plant the whole range of vegetables except sweet potatoes; set out asparagus, onion sets and strawberry plants.

*October*—Plant same as last month; put in garden peas; set out cabbage plants; dig sweet potatoes; sow oats, rye, etc.

*November*—A good month for garden; continue to plant and transplant, same as for October; sow oats, barley and rye for winter pasturage crops; dig sweet potatoes; house or bank them; make sugar and syrup.

*December*—Clear up generally; fence, ditch, manure, and plant hardy vegetables; plant, set out orange trees, fruit trees and shrubbery; keep a sharp look-out for an occasional frost; a slight protection will prevent injury.

It will be seen from the above, that there is no month in the year but what fresh and growing vegetables can be had for sale and domestic use.

A single season will afford strawberries from the setting out, ripe figs from two-year-old cuttings, grapes the second year, peaches the second and third years, oranges from the bud in three to five years.

The region for miles about Tarpon Springs is particularly adapted to all citrus products.

A party of gentlemen who were there last spring have bonded a tract of 1,000 acres with a view of forming a stock company for raising vegetables and semi-tropical fruits to ship north. Orange will be the ultimate result. The whole will be laid out in one gorgeous system of Oranges, Lemons, Guavers, Bananas, Figs, etc. But from the immense profits in vegetables, and that they may utilize the winter and summer alike, it is to be an orange and vegetable company at the same time.

# TEMPERATURE OF FLORIDA.

This page is for the intelligent. It has seemed to be a difficult thing to comprehend the summers of Florida. I find many supposing that, as the Florida winters were warmer than our winters, its summers must be correspondingly warmer than our summers. After reading this, never say or think so again. It would show your incompetency to comprehend the very simple table below.

Table of temperatures taken at Tallahassee, the capital, showing the average temperature for June, during three successive years.

|  | Monthly mean at 7 a. m. | Monthly mean at 2 p. m. | Monthly mean at 9 a. m. | Monthly means. |
|---|---|---|---|---|
| June, 1881............................. | 80.0 | 89.8 | 84.5 | 84.8 |
| " 1882............................. | 77.1 | 86.1 | 78.4 | 80.5 |
| " 1883............................. | 78.9 | 87.2 | 78.3 | 81.4 |

The better and truer idea of Florida may be had by saying that its summers are a continuation of its enjoyable winters. There are a few isolated locations which are exceptions to this as to all other good rules. For instance, at the extreme southern point around the swamp lands of the everglades, where fevers are created, and also on the St. John's River, and at Jacksonville, most delightful places in the winter, are not so in summer. In this then is what the western coast—that bordering on the Gulf of Mexico—excels. The whole expression of this location may be implied by the remark a gentleman from New York made, who had been at Tarpon Springs at two different times—February and September. "Why!" said he, "one might come here in the winter to get rid of the cold; and in the summer to get rid of the heat of the north." This remark, however, can be applied only, we must recollect, where a place has the advantage of the breezes, and purifying element of lakes and the other water systems which exists in Florida.

## ROUTE TO THE WEST COAST.

The West coast, which has heretofore lain a hidden pleasure waste to most every condition of the sportsman, has now a practical source of access in the new steamboat, "Gov. Safford," which has been put on to ply down the west coast from Cedar Keys. Heretofore parties could go only as far as Cedar Keys with that comfort and luxury which betokens the American, and there held in abeyance by the tantalizing stories of the achievements of the "fly" and the gun; with the phantom vision of mystic lakes, the safe bayous, and streams teaming with the choicest specimens of the finny tribe which lined the coast to the south, and then return home without seeing that part of Florida which has aroused both the avarice and curiosity of all for the past few years.

This location has been extolled by every one who has seen it since the Spaniards first besought their King in 1539 to " lay hold and possess it." ·

The routes to the two entry ports of Florida—Fernandina and Jacksonville—are so numerous, persons have now an almost unlimited choice, both by land or water. All persons from either the North or West buy their tickets to either one of these two points. From here let us suggest a route and then indulge in a few remarks.

# The Great New Route Through Florida

THIS SEASON IS,

## Arriving at Fernandina or Jacksonville from New York,

TO TAKE

| THE | FROM | TO | DISTANCE |
|---|---|---|---|
| Florida Railway and Navigation Company. | Jacksonville or Fernandina. | Cedar Keys, | 155 miles. |
| New and splendid Steamer " Governor Safford." | Cedar Keys | Tarpon Springs, and down the Coast to Anclote, Dunedin, Disston and Tampa. | About 100 miles. |
| South Florida Railway. | Tampa | Sanford. | 115 miles. |
| St. John's River Boats. | Sanford | Jacksonville or Fernandina. | 193 miles. |

The foregoing table gives a route to tourists visiting Florida by which they can see more of the State, and at less cost than any other trip of equal length he can make in all Florida. He first crosses the Northern part of the State through that section, which portrays that condition of climate which is just sufficiently removed from the climate of the southern portion of the State, to prevent the production of some of the more tropical fruits.

The steamer "Gov. Safford" will then escort you through a region possessing conditions for every variety of pleasure known.

The trip across the South Florida Railroad to Sanford takes you through the more tropical Florida; while

The trip from Sanford to Jacksonville takes you down the wonderful St. John's to Jacksonville, and completes a trip which you will be sure to repeat the next season. This whole circuit, from Jacksonville throughout the state, and return to Jacksonville without doubling any ground can, at the present high prices, be made for $25. We can not presume to give the exact cost as there is all probability of there being a reduction from time to time hereafter, with the rapidly increasing facilities. This will, however, guide you in your rough calculations for this winter.

AN EXCURSION WILL LEAVE

# New York for Florida

AT

# Very Reduced Rates.

## ON JANUARY 15TH, 1885.

This Excursion will be the first to take in the

# NEWLY OPENED COUNTRY,

AND THE

# Rich Orange Fields of the West Coast of Florida.

The route will be that suggested on page 32 of this pamphlet. As one will see this route exhibits to the traveler, not only all

## The Principal Cities of the South,

But also the different Geographical and

## Climatic Features of Florida.

It takes in

## THE BEAUTIFUL ST. JOHN'S.

It shows you the Orange Lands of the West Coast of Florida. It traverses the Highlands of North-Central Florida, and charms you with the Semi-tropical growth of Southern Florida. It gives you at

## TARPON SPRINGS

YACHTING AND FISHING, SUCH AS THE

SPORTSMEN NEVER DREAMED OF.

# COME AND ENJOY
## THAT EXHILARATING CHANGE
### FROM SHADOW INTO SUNSHINE!
### FROM STERILE NORTH to SUNNY SOUTH!

The Excursion will leave foot of Cortland (or Desbrosses) Streets on January 15th, and take in Washington;' Richmond; Wilmington; Charlestown; Savannah; Jacksonville; Cedar Keys; Tarpon Springs; Tampa; Sanford; Palatka; St. John's River.

Come to Florida ! thy wise and better sage,
And plant thy grove before you are to old.
For, as the sun brings priceless gifts to youth,
The *Golden Fruit* will line your tills with *Gold*.

# A LEADING FEATURE
of this trip will be

## A SPECIAL EXCURSION
# FROM TARPON SPRINGS TO TAMPA.

Where all will have an opportunity of visiting the grand new summer hotel

# "THE PALMETTO,"
Just opened at Tampa.

# ORANGES AND BANANAS

are ripe in December and January, and may be picked from tree and bush.

The Boom in Florida has begun.
Take it in, the bud!

For rates, special privileges for stopping off, and all other information concerning the trip, apply to

## H. CONKLIN,
*196 Broadway, Room 20, New York.*

# PROSPECTUS OF THE
# TARPON FRUIT AND LAND COMPANY.

## SOME FACTS ABOUT FLORIDA.

The great influx to Florida for the past two years has awakened an unprecedented interest in all the industries; and Florida shows to-day, that life, which California did in '49. California for her gold; but Florida for her more permanent golden fruits.

Within the past two years Florida has increased her Railroad facilities from two distinct lines to fifty projected ones, and

## TEN NEW ROADS IN ACTUAL OPERATION.

Fourteen thousand families settled in Florida last year, '83. These were actual settlers and have no reference to the tens-of-thousands tourists and travelers who visit there every year.

More conspicuous than the other industries now obtaining there, is that of fruit and vegetables growing. When we speak of this as an *industry* we speak of it as a commercial interest, and not as an individual farm. Companies are forming over all the state for the production of fruits and vegetables, for shipment North during the winter months, and the fabulous prices realized from this industry, yet in its infancy, bespeaks the future.

## THE
# Tarpon Fruit and Land Company,

The objects of this company are the growing of fruits and vegetables all the year round and shipping North during the winter months.

The practibility of, and the profits in, such an enterprise can be got from any and all published matter on Florida.

The company has bonded a tract of one thousand acres of orange land on the North side of the Cootee River, Florida. The Cootee, which has had its name boiled down from *Pithlachuscootee*, is a beautiful stream running directly west and emptying into the Gulf of Mexico, and at whose mouth is Port Richie. South of this is the equally beautiful Anclote River, only six miles apart, running parallel, and also emptying into the Gulf of Mexico. At the North of this river is located the famous Watering Place and Summer Resort of

# TARPON SPRINGS.

The company's lands are located on the Cootee, about three miles from its mouth, and the river is navigable for some distance above the lands.

From the above facts it will be seen these have two points of shipment. First, directly down the Cootee river to Port Richie, three miles. Secondly, by wagon down to the Anclote River and Tarpon Springs. At both these places, the Gulf Coast Steamboat Company, opened in November, '84, transports freight to Cedar Keys and all parts of the country direct. This company offers a new feature to each one of its incorporators. It deeds at once a 5-acre tract, beautifully located for a winter residence in Florida.

No other company offers this great inducement.

Three more of ten incorporators are wanted.

---

# THE EXCURSION

### WHICH LEAVES NEW YORK

## ON THE 15th OF JANUARY,

### WILL GO OVER THE GROUNDS.

Take the Trip and see the Country for Yourself.

For further information, address,

## E. CONKLIN,

*196 BROADWAY, Room 20, NEW YORK.*

# THIS SPACE IS RESERVED

# FOR AN ENGRAVING

OF THE

## "PALMETTO"

## THE MAGNIFICENT NEW HOTEL

Situated at the Head of Tampa Bay.

---

# THE

# "PALMETTO."

THE

## Winter and Summer Resort

OF

# FLORIDA.

H. L. SCRANTON,                    Proprietor

# The "Suwanee"

## THE ONLY STRICTLY

# TOURISTS' HOTEL,

### AT

# CEDAR KEYS, FLORIDA.

OYSTERS AND FISH A SPECIALTY.

# The St. James

## THE

# LEADING HOTEL,

### IN

# JACKSONVILLE, FLORIDA,

J. R. CAMPBELL, - - PROPRIETOR.

# THE INAUGURATION

OF THE STEAMER

# "GOVERNOR SAFFORD"

Nov. 1884.

### PLYING BETWEEN

# CEDAR KEYS AND DISSTON

ON THE

# West Coast of Florida

Was the opening up to the world of that section of Florida, which will be

### THE GREAT

# YACHTING AND FISHING GROUNDS

## OF THE SOUTH EAST.

---

Hear what a correspondent of the *New York Herald* said of a trip up the coast last winter:

"Tampa Bay was then visited, which stretch of water was left on April 8th, for the fishing grounds between Egmont Key and Cedar Keys. The run to the northward was very pleasant, and the fishing found to be excellent. The yachtsmen speak in the highest praise of the west coast of Florida as a yachting ground. Fine harbors are to be found every ten or fifteen miles, the water is smooth, the storms or squalls are rare. The fishing and shooting are excellent, and nowhere so far as observation extends, can be found more enjoyable waters for genuine yachting, comfort and amusement.

—TO—

# Florida, New Orleans, Texas, Mexico, &c.,

Remember that this is the only Route running

# 3 SOUTHERN EXPRESS TRAINS DAILY 3

That it is the only Route Running Through

## Pullman Palace Buffet Sleeping Cars,

# NEW YORK TO JACKSONVILLE,

And the only Route Passing through the Cities of

# Richmond, Wilmington, Charleston & Savannah.

For tickets, time tables, reservation of Sleeping Car, Sections and Berths,
apply at following named offices:

NEW ORLEANS; 102 CANAL STREET.
MARION KNOWLES, Passenger Agent, Savannah, Ga.
JNO. H. GRIFFEN, Passenger Agent, or WM. BRIEN, 22 Bull St.
JACKSONVILLE; Ticket Office, WAY CROSS SHORT LINE, Astor Build'g.
FLORIDA HEADQUARTERS, 261 BROADWAY, New York.

## H. C. HARDEN,
*Eastern Passenger Agent.*

## C. D. OWENS,
*General Agent.*

# A MAN

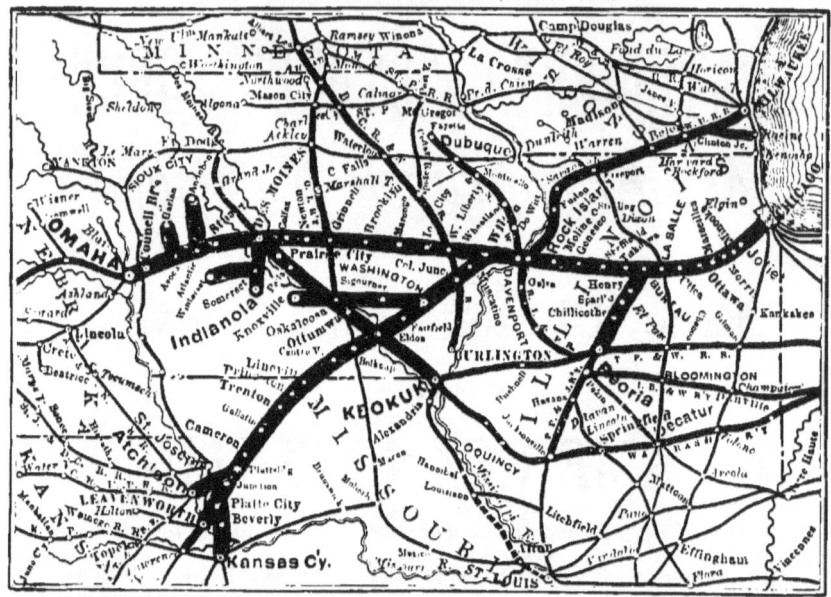

## CHICAGO, ROCK ISLAND & PACIFIC R. R.

IS THE GREAT CONNECTING LINK BETWEEN THE EAST AND THE WEST!

AND AT SAN FRANCISCO WITH THE

## SUPERB STEAMER "CALIFORNIA."

FOR ALL POINTS IN

## Washington Territory, Oregon and Alaska.

THE STEAMER "CALIFORNIA."

Running between San Francisco and all points in Washington Territory, Oregon and Alaska.

# NOW OPEN.

## THE NEW ROUTE BETWEEN

## CEDAR KEY AND DISSTON

### ON THE

# West Coast of Florida.

### The New and Commodious STEAMER

# "GOVERNOR SAFFORD,"

### is now making regular trips between

# CEDAR KEY and DISSTON,

### INCLUDING

## Hudson, Anclote, Tarpon Springs, Port Richie,

## Dunedin, Clear Water Harbor and Disston.

All visitors to Florida, will hail this new route, as it has been the clamor of tourists to Florida for some time back to visit the great natural Yachting and Fishing grounds, known to exist in this section.

Leaving Cedar Key one day, and returning the next, gives all a daylight view of this heretofore unknown, but choicest portion of Florida.

## *Take this ride and stop off at the Beautiful*

## TARPON SPRINGS.